The Philosophy of the Short-Story

Brander Matthews

Philosophy of the Short-story

By

Brander Matthews, D. C. L.
Professor of Dramatic Literature in Columbia University

Longmans, Green, and Co.
91 and 93 Fifth Avenue, New York
London and Bombay
1901

First Edition, January, 1901
Reprinted, April, 1901

UNIVERSITY PRESS · JOHN WILSON
AND SON · CAMBRIDGE, U.S.A.

To my Friend and Colleague

HARRY THURSTON PECK

Prefatory Note

CERTAIN of the opinions put forward in the following pages were first expressed briefly (and anonymously) in the columns of the *Saturday Review* of London in the summer of 1884. The present paper, in which these opinions were more elaborately set forth, and with a greater variety of illustration, was originally printed in *Lippincott's Magazine* for October, 1885. After a while it was included in a volume called 'Pen and Ink: Essays on subjects of more or less importance,' published in the fall of 1888 (New York and London: Longmans, Green, & Co).

In the final ten years of the nineteenth century an increasing attention has been paid to the history of fiction and to the principles of narrative art. In many of the leading American universities the modern novel has been serving as the subject for lectures and as the material for private study, in the course of which the Short-story received a fair share of consideration. No doubt, it is in consequence of this incessant discussion of modern fiction and of its methods that the author and the publishers have been made aware of a demand for the present essay, with such revision and annotation as might render it more useful, not only to the earnest student, but also to the casual reader.

B. M.

COLUMBIA UNIVERSITY.
January 1, 1901.

Contents

The Philosophy of the Short-story

I

IF it chance that artists fall to talking about their art, it is the critic's place to listen, that he may pick up a little knowledge. Of late, certain of the novelists of Great Britain and the United States have been discussing the principles and the practice of the art of writing stories. Mr. Howells declared his warm appreciation of Mr. Henry James's novels; Mr. Stevenson made public a delightful plea for Romance; Mr. Besant lectured gracefully on the Art of Fiction; and Mr. James modestly presented his views by way of supplement and criticism.[1] The discussion took a wide range. With more or less fulness it covered the proper aim and intent of the novelist, his material and his methods, his success, his rewards, social and pecuniary, and the morality of his work and of his art. But, with all its extension, the discussion did not include one important branch of the art of fiction: it did not consider at all the minor art of the

[1] Mr. Besant's lecture was published in a pamphlet (London: Chatto and Windus). Mr. James's essay may be found in his 'Partial Portraits' (London and New York: Macmillan & Co). Mr. Stevenson's 'Humble Remonstrance,' as well as his cognate 'Gossip on Romance,' are included in the volume called 'Memories and Portraits' (New York: Scribner; London: Chatto and Windus). The substance of Mr. Howells's doctrines can be found succinctly set forth in his little book called 'Criticism and Fiction' (New York: Harper & Brothers).

Short-story. Although neither Mr. Howells nor Mr. James, Mr. Besant nor Mr. Stevenson specifically limited his remarks to those longer, and, in the picture-dealer's sense of the word, more "important," tales known as Novels, and although, of course, their general criticisms of the abstract principles of the art of fiction applied quite as well to the Short-story as to the Novel, yet all their concrete examples were full-length Novels; and the Short-story, as such, received no recognition at all.

[And here occasion serves to record with regret the fact that even in the more recent volumes on the history of fiction published since the original appearance of the present essay in 1885, — valuable as they are and most welcome to all lovers of literature, — there is a strange neglect of the Short-story.

The relation of the Short-story to the Novel, and the influence which the one may at any time have exerted upon the development of the other, — these are topics not taken up in Professor Walter Raleigh's 'The English Novel,' or in Professor W. L. Cross's 'Development of the English Novel,' or in Professor F. H. Stoddard's 'Evolution of the English Novel.' They are not discussed even in Mr. Henry Wilson's annotated edition of Dunlop's 'History of Prose Fiction,' in which there is a genuine effort to consider all the aspects of the art of the story-teller.]

II

THE difference between a Novel and a Novelet is one of length only: a Novelet is a brief Novel. But the difference between a Novel and a Short-story is a difference of kind. A true Short-story is something other and something more than a mere story which is short. A true Short-story differs from the Novel chiefly in its essential unity of impression. In a far more exact and precise use of the word, a Short-story has unity as a Novel cannot have it.[1] Often, it may

[1] In a letter to a friend, Stevenson lays down the law with his usual directness: "Make another end to it? Ah, yes, but that's not the way I write; the whole tale is implied; I never use an effect when I

be noted by the way, the Short-story fulfils the three false unities of the French classic drama: it shows one action, in one place, on one day. A Short-story deals with a single character, a single event, a single emotion, or the series of emotions called forth by a single situation. Poe's paradox[1] that a poem cannot greatly exceed a hundred lines in length under penalty

can help it, unless it prepares the effects that are to follow; that 's what a story consists in. To make another end, that is to make the beginning all wrong. The *dénouement* of a long story is nothing, it is just 'a full close,' which you may approach and accompany as you please — it is a coda, not an essential member in the rhythm; but the body and end of a short-story is bone of the bone and blood of the blood of the beginning." 'Vailima Letters,' vol. i., p. 147.

[1] See his essay on 'The Philosophy of Composition,' to be found in the sixth volume of the collected edition of his works, prepared by Messrs. Stedman and Woodberry.

of ceasing to be one poem and breaking into a string of poems, may serve to suggest the precise difference between the Short-story and the Novel. The Short-story is the single effect, complete and self-contained, while the Novel is of necessity broken into a series of episodes. Thus the Short-story has, what the Novel cannot have, the effect of "totality," as Poe called it, the unity of impression.

Of a truth the Short-story is not only not a chapter out of a Novel, or an incident or an episode extracted from a longer tale, but at its best it impresses the reader with the belief that it would be spoiled if it were made larger, or if it were incorporated into a more elaborate work. The difference in spirit and in form between the Lyric and the Epic is scarcely greater than the difference between the Short-story and the Novel; and the 'Raven' and 'How we brought the good news from Ghent to Aix' are not more unlike the 'Lady of the Lake' and 'Paradise Lost,' in form and in spirit, than the 'Luck of Roaring Camp,' and the 'Man without a Country,' two typical Short-stories, are unlike 'Vanity Fair' and the 'Heart of Midlothian,' two typical Novels.

Another great difference between the Short-story and the Novel lies in the fact that the Novel, nowadays at least, must be a love-tale, while the Short-story need not deal with love at all. Although there are to be found by diligent search a few Novels which are not love-tales — and of course 'Robinson Crusoe' is the example that swims at once into recollection — yet the immense majority of Novels have the tender passion either as the motive power of their machinery or as the pivot on which their plots turn. Although 'Vanity Fair' was a Novel without a hero, nearly every other Novel has a hero and a heroine; and the novelist, however unwillingly, must concern himself in their love-affairs.

But the writer of Short-stories is under no bonds of this sort. Of course he may tell a tale of love if he choose, and if love enters into his tale naturally and to its enriching; but he need not bother with love at all unless he please. Some of the best of Short-stories are love-stories too, — Mr. Aldrich's 'Margery Daw,' for instance, Mr. Stimson's 'Mrs. Knollys,' Mr. Bunner's 'Love in Old Cloathes'; but more of them are not love-stories at all. If we were to pick out the ten best Short-stories, I think we should find that fewer than half of them made any mention at all of love. In the 'Snow Image' and in the 'Ambitious Guest,' in the 'Gold Bug' and in the 'Fall of the House of Usher,' in 'My Double, and how he Undid me,' in 'Devil-Puzzlers,' in the 'Outcasts of Poker Flat,' in 'Jean-ah Poquelin,' in 'A Bundle of Letters,' there is little or no mention of the love of man for woman, which is generally the chief topic of conversation in a Novel.

While the Novel cannot get on easily without love, the Short-story can. Since love seems to be almost the only thing which will give interest to a long story, the writer of Novels has to get love into his tales as best he may, even when the subject rebels and when he himself is too old to take any delight in the mating of John and Joan. But the Short-story, being brief, does not need a love-interest to hold its parts together, and the writer of Short-stories has thus a greater freedom; he may do as he pleases; from him a love-tale is not expected.[1]

[1] In an essay on 'The Local Short-story' contributed to the *Independent* for March 11, 1892, Colonel T. W. Higginson points out the disadvantages the novelist labours under when he knows that his work is to be published in instalments; and he declares that this possible serial publication "affords the justification of the short-story. For here, at least, we have the conditions of perfect art; there is no sub-division of interest; the author can strike directly in, without preface, can move with determined step toward a conclusion, and can — O highest privilege! — stop when he is done. For the most perfect examples of the short-story — those of De Maupassant, for instance — the reader feels, if he can pause to think, that they must have been done at a sitting, so complete is the grasp, the single grasp, upon the

But other things are required of a writer of Short-stories which are not required of a writer of Novels. The novelist may take his time; he has abundant room to turn about. The writer of Short-stories must be concise, and compression, a vigorous compression, is essential. For him, more than

mind. This completeness secures the end; they need not be sensational, because there is no necessity of keeping up a series of exciting minor incidents; the main incident is enough. Around the very centre of motion, as in a whirlwind, there may be a perfect quiet, a quiet which is formidable in its very repose. In De Maupassant's terrific story of Corsican vengeance, 'Une Vendetta,' in which the sole actor is a lonely old woman who trains a fierce dog so that he ultimately kills her enemy, the author simply tells us, at the end, that this quiet fiend of destruction went peacefully home and went to sleep. *Elle dormit bien, cette nuit-là.* The cyclone has spent itself, and the silence it has left behind it is more formidable than the cyclone."

for any one else, the half is more than the whole. Again, the novelist may be commonplace, he may bend his best energies to the photographic reproduction of the actual; if he show us a cross-section of real life we are content; but the writer of Short-stories must have originality and ingenuity. If to compression, originality, and ingenuity he add also a touch of fantasy, so much the better.

In fact, it may be said that no one has ever succeeded as a writer of Short-stories who had not ingenuity, originality, and compression; and that most of those who have succeeded in this line had also the touch of fantasy. But there are not a few successful novelists lacking, not only in fantasy and compression, but also in ingenuity and originality; they had other qualities, no doubt, but these they had not. If an example must be given, the name of Anthony Trollope will occur to all. Fantasy was a thing he abhorred; compression he knew not; and originality and ingenuity can be conceded to him only by a strong stretch of the ordinary meaning of the words. Other qualities he had in plenty, but not these. And, not having them, he was not a writer of Short-stories. Judging from his essay on Hawthorne,[1] one may even go so far as to say that Trollope did not know a good Short-story when he saw it.

I have written "Short-stories" with a

[1] This critical paper of Trollope's on 'The Genius of Nathaniel Hawthorne' was contributed to the *North American Review* for September, 1879. Apparently, like many other of his essays, it has not been reprinted.

capital S and a hyphen because I wished to emphasise the distinction between the Short-story and the story which is merely short. The Short-story is a high and difficult department of fiction. The story which is short can be written by anybody who can write at all; and it may be good, bad, or indifferent; but at its best it is wholly unlike the Short-story. In 'An Editor's Tales' Trollope has given us excellent specimens of the story which is short; and the narratives which make up this book are amusing enough and clever enough, but they are wanting in the individuality and in the completeness of the genuine Short-story. Like the brief tales to be seen in the British monthly magazines and in the Sunday editions of American newspapers into which they are copied, they are, for the most part, either merely amplified anecdotes or else incidents which might have been used in a Novel just as well as not.

Now, it cannot be said too emphatically that the genuine Short-story abhors the idea of the Novel. It neither can be conceived as part of a Novel, nor can it be elaborated and expanded so as to form a Novel. A good Short-story is no more the synopsis of a Novel than it is an episode from a Novel.[1] A slight Novel, or a Novel cut down, is a Novelet: it is not a

[1] In some rambling notes on "The Short-story" contributed to the *Nineteenth Century* for March, 1898, Mr. Frederick Wedmore reiterates certain of the points made in this essay. For one thing, he declares that a good Short-story can never be 'a novel in a nut-shell'; it "cannot possibly be a *précis*, a synopsis, a *scenario*, as it were, of a novel. It is a separate thing — as separate, almost, as the Sonnet is from the Epic, — it involves the exercise almost of a different art."

Short-story. Mr. Howells's 'Their Wedding Journey' and Miss Howard's 'One Summer' are Novelets,—little Novels. Mr. Anstey's 'Vice Versa,' Mr. Besant's 'Case of Mr. Lucraft,' Hugh Conway's 'Called Back,' Mr. Julian Hawthorne's 'Archibald Malmaison,' and Mr. Stevenson's 'Strange Case of Dr. Jekyll and Mr. Hyde' are Short-stories in conception, although they are without the compression which the Short-story requires.

It may be remembered that in the acute and learned essay on *vers de société* which he prefixed to his admirable 'Lyra Elegantiarum,' Mr. Frederick Locker declared that the two characteristics of the best *vers de société* were brevity and brilliancy, and that the 'Rape of the Lock' would be the type and model of the best *vers de société*—if it were not just a little too long. So it is with the 'Case of Mr. Lucraft,' with 'Vice Versa,' with 'Archibald Malmaison': they are just a little too long.

III

It is to be noted as a curious coincidence that there is no exact word in English to designate either *vers de société* or the Short-story, and yet in no language are there better *vers de société* or Short-stories than in English. It may be remarked also that there is a certain likeness between *vers de société* and Short-stories: for one thing, both seem easy to write and are hard. And the typical qualifications of each may apply with almost equal force to the other: *vers de société* should reveal compression, ingenuity, and originality, and Short-stories should have brevity and brilliancy. In no class of writing are neatness of construction and polish of execution more needed than in the writing of *vers de société* and of Short-stories. The writer of Short-stories must have the sense of form, which has well been called "the highest and last attribute of a creative writer." The construction must always be logical, adequate, harmonious.

Here is the weak spot in Mr. W. H. Bishop's 'One of the Thirty Pieces,' the fundamental idea of which — that fatality awaits every successive possessor of every one of the coins once paid to Judas for his betrayal of Jesus — has genuine strength, not fully developed in the story. But other of Mr. Bishop's stories — the 'Battle of Bunkerloo,' for instance — are admirable in all ways, conception and execution having an even excellence. Again, Hugh Conway's 'Daughter of the Stars' is a Short-story which fails from sheer deficiency of style: here is one of the very finest Short-story ideas — the startling and fascinating fantasy that by sheer force of will a man might have been able to draw down from the depths of the sky a lovely astral maid to share his finite human life — ever given to any mortal, but the handling is at best barely sufficient. To do justice to the conception would tax the execution of a poet. We could merely wonder what the tale would have been had it occurred to Hawthorne, to Poe, or to Théophile Gautier. An idea logically developed by one possessing the sense of form and the gift of style is what we look for in the Short-story.

But, although the sense of form and the gift of style are essential to the writing of a good Short-story, they are secondary to the idea, to the conception, to the subject. Those who hold, with a certain American novelist, that it is no matter what you have to say, but only how you say it, need not attempt the Short-story; for the Short-story, far more than the Novel even, demands a subject. The Short-story is nothing if there is no story to tell; — one might almost say that a Short-story is nothing if it has no plot, — except that "plot" may suggest to some readers a complication and an elaboration which are not really needful. But a plan — if this word is less liable to misconception than "plot" — a plan a Short-story must have, while it would be easy to cite Novels of eminence which are wholly amorphous — for example, 'Tristram Shandy.'

Whatever its length, the Novel, so Mr. Henry James told us not long ago, "is, in its broadest definition, a personal impression of life." The most powerful force in French fiction to-day is M. Émile Zola, chiefly known in America and England, I fear me greatly, by the dirt which masks and degrades the real beauty and firm strength not seldom concealed in his novels; and M. Émile Zola declares that the novelist of the future will not concern himself with the artistic evolution of a plot: he will take *une histoire quelconque*, any kind of a story, and make it serve his purpose,—which is to give elaborate pictures of life in all its most minute details.

It is needless to say that the acceptance of these theories is a negation of the Short-story. Important as are form and style, the subject of the Short-story is of more importance yet. What you have to tell is of greater interest than how you tell it. I once heard a clever American novelist pour sarcastic praise upon another American novelist, — for novelists, even American novelists, do not always dwell together in unity. The subject of the eulogy was the chief of those who had come to be known as the International Novelists; and he was praised because he had invented and made possible a fifth plot. Hitherto, declared the eulogist, only four terminations of a novel have been known to the most enthusiastic and untiring student of fiction. First, they are married; or second, she marries some one else; or, thirdly, he marries some one else; or fourthly, and lastly, she dies. Now, continued the panegyrist, a fifth termination has been shown to be practicable: they are not married, she does not die, he does not die, — and nothing happens at all. As a Short-story need not be a love-story, it is of no consequence at all whether they marry or die; but a Short-story in which nothing happens at all is an absolute impossibility.

Perhaps the difference between a Short-story and a Sketch can best be indicated by saying that, while a Sketch may be still-life, in a Short-story something always happens. A Sketch may be an outline of character, or even a picture of a mood of mind, but in a Short-story there must be something done, there must be an action.[1] Yet the dis-

[1] This difference is considered briefly by Mr. F. B. Perkins in the characteristically clever preface to the volume of his ingenious Short-stories, which takes its title from the first and best — 'Devil-Puzzlers' (New York: G. P. Putnam's Sons).

tinction, like that between the Novel and the Romance, is no longer of vital importance. In the preface to the 'House of the Seven Gables,' Hawthorne sets forth the difference between the Novel and the Romance, and claims for himself the privileges of the romancer. Mr. Henry James [1] fails to see this difference. The fact is, that the Short-story and the Sketch, the Novel and the Romance, melt and merge one into the other, and no man may mete the boundaries of each, though their extremes lie far apart. With the more complete understanding of the principle of development and evolution in literary art, as in physical nature, we see the futility of a strict and rigid classification into pre-

[1] In the narrow but suggestive biography of Hawthorne contributed to Mr. John Morley's 'English Men of Letters.'

cisely defined genera and species. All that is needful for us to remark now is that the Short-story has limitless possibilities: it may be as realistic as the most prosaic novel, or as fantastic as the most ethereal romance.

IV

As a touch of fantasy, however slight, is a welcome ingredient in a Short-story, and as the American takes more thought of things unseen than the Englishman, we may have here an incomplete explanation of the superiority of the American Short-story over the British. "John Bull has suffered the idea of the Invisible to be very much fattened out of him," says Mr. Lowell: "Jonathan is conscious still that he lives in the World of the Unseen as well as of the Seen." It is not enough to catch a ghost white-handed and to hale him into the full glare of the electric light. A brutal misuse of the supernatural is perhaps the very lowest degradation of the art of fiction. But "to mingle the marvellous rather as a slight, delicate, and evanescent flavour than as any actual portion of the substance," to quote from the preface to the 'House of the Seven Gables,' this is, or should be, the aim of the writer of Short-stories whenever his feet leave the firm ground of fact as he strays in the unsubstantial realms of fantasy.

In no one's writings, it seems to me, is this better exemplified than in Hawthorne's,—not even in Poe's. There is a propriety in Hawthorne's fantasy to which Poe could not attain. Hawthorne's effects are moral, where Poe's are merely physical. The situation and its logical development, and the effects to be got out of it, are all Poe thinks of. In Hawthorne the situation, however strange and weird, is only the outward and visible sign of an inward and spiritual struggle. Ethical consequences are always worrying Hawthorne's soul: but Poe did not know that there were any ethics.

There are literary evolutionists who, in their whim of seeing in every original writer a copy of some predecessor, have declared that Hawthorne is derived from Tieck, and Poe from Hoffmann, just as Dickens modelled himself on Smollett, and Thackeray followed in the footsteps of Fielding. In all four cases the pupil surpassed the master,—if haply Tieck and Hoffmann can be considered as even remotely the masters of Hawthorne and Poe. When Coleridge was told that Klopstock was the German Milton, he assented with the dry addendum, "A very German Milton." So is Hoffmann a very German Poe;

and Tieck, at best, is only a very German Hawthorne.

In fact, both Poe and Hawthorne are as American as any one can be. If the adjective American has any meaning at all, it qualifies Poe and Hawthorne. They were American to the core. They both revealed the curious sympathy with Oriental moods of thought which is often an American characteristic. Poe, with his cold logic and his mathematical analysis, and Hawthorne, with his introspective conscience and his love of the subtile and the invisible, are representative of phases of American character not to be mistaken by any one who has given thought to the influence of nationality.

As to which of the two was the greater, discussion is idle; but that Hawthorne was the finer genius, few would deny. Poe,[1] as cunning an artificer of goldsmith's-work and as adroit in its vending as was ever M. Josse, declared that "Hawthorne's distinctive trait is invention, creation, imagination, originality, — a trait which in the literature of fiction is positively worth all the rest." But with the moral basis of Hawthorne's work, which had flowered in the crevices and crannies of New England Puritanism, Poe did not concern himself. In Poe's hands the story of the 'Ambitious Guest' might have

[1] In his review of Hawthorne's earlier tales, contributed originally to *Graham's Magazine*, and to be consulted now in the seventh volume of the critical edition prepared by Messrs. Stedman and Woodberry. It is both interesting and instructive to compare this article on Hawthorne in which Poe vaunts the superiority of the Short-story over the Novel, with the paper on the 'Philosophy of Composition,' in which he makes a similar claim for the Lyric over the Epic.

thrilled us with a more powerful horror, but it would have lacked the ethical beauty which Hawthorne gave it and which makes it significant beyond a mere feat of verbal legerdemain. And the subtile simplicity of the 'Great Stone Face' is as far from Poe as the pathetic irony of the 'Ambitious Guest.' In all his most daring fantasies Hawthorne is natural; and, though he may project his vision far beyond the boundaries of fact, nowhere does he violate the laws of nature. He had at all times a wholesome simplicity, and he never showed any trace of the morbid taint which characterises nearly all Poe's work. Hawthorne, one may venture to say, had the broad sanity of genius, while we should understand any one who might declare that Poe had mental disease raised to the nth.

Although it may be doubted whether the fiery and tumultuous rush of a volcano, which might be taken to typify Poe, is as powerful or impressive in the end as the calm and inevitable progression of a glacier, to which, for the purposes of this comparison only, we may liken Hawthorne, yet the weight and influence of Poe's work are indisputable. One might hazard the assertion that in all Latin countries he is the best known of American authors. Certainly no American writer has been so widely accepted in France. Nothing better of its kind has ever been done than the 'Pit and the Pendulum,' or than the 'Fall of the House of Usher' (which has been compared aptly with Browning's 'Childe Roland to the Dark Tower came' for its power of suggesting intellectual desolation). Nothing better of its kind has ever been done than the 'Gold Bug,' or than the 'Purloined Letter,' or than the 'Murders in the Rue Morgue.'

The 'Murders in the Rue Morgue' is indeed a story of the most marvellous skill: it was the first of its kind, and to this day it remains a model, not only unsurpassed, but unapproachable.[1] It was the first of detective stories; and it has had thousands of imitations and no rival. The originality, the ingenuity, the verisimilitude of this tale and of its fellows are beyond all praise. Poe had a faculty which one may call imaginative

[1] For example, it is not unfair to suggest that all the manifold feats of Dr. Conan Doyle's very clever 'Sherlock Holmes' are latent in one or another of these tales of Poe's, — M. Dupin being the prototype of Holmes himself, and the autobiographic narrator standing in the same attitude of wondering admiration that Dr. Watson takes in the British series.

ratiocination to a degree beyond all other writers of fiction.[1] He did not at all times keep up to the high level, in one style, of the 'Fall of the House of Usher,' and, in another, of the 'Murders in the Rue Morgue,' and it was not to be expected that he should. Only too often did he sink to the grade of the ordinary 'Tale from *Blackwood*,' which he himself satirised in his usual savage vein of humour.

And yet there is no denying that even in his flimsiest and most tawdry tales we see the truth of Mr. Lowell's

[1] In his very suggestive study of Poe in 'New Essays toward a critical method,' Mr. J. M. Robertson quotes from the Spanish critic Landa the statement that Poe "has been the first story-writer to exploit the field of science in the department of the marvellous;" and he has further been the first "to exploit the marvellous in morbid psychology with scientific art" (p. 103).

assertion that Poe had "two of the prime qualities of genius, — a faculty of vigorous yet minute analysis, and a wonderful fecundity of imagination." Mr. Loweil said also that Poe combined "in a very remarkable manner two faculties which are seldom found united, — a power of influencing the mind of the reader by the impalpable shadows of mystery, and a minuteness of detail which does not leave a pin or a button unnoticed. Both are, in truth, the natural results of the predominating quality of his mind, to which we have before alluded, — analysis."[1] In Poe's hands, however, the enumeration of pins and buttons, the

[1] It is to be regretted that Lowell's acute criticism of Poe is not to be found in the complete edition of his own works, but only in an early and incomplete edition of Poe's.

exact imitation of the prosaic facts of humdrum life in this workaday world, is not an end, but a means only, whereby he constructs and intensifies the shadow of mystery which broods over the things thus realistically portrayed.

V

WITH the recollection that it is more than half a century since Hawthorne and Poe wrote their best Short-stories, it is not a little comic to see now and again in American newspapers a rash assertion that "American literature has hitherto been deficient in good Short-stories," or the reckless declaration that "the art of writing Short-stories has not hitherto been cultivated in the United States."[1] Nothing could be more inexact than these statements. Almost as soon as America began to

[1] The reader may be reminded once more that this essay was written in 1885. Although these absurd assertions were not infrequent then, they are unknown now.

have any literature at all it had good Short-stories.[1] It is quite within ten, or at the most twenty, years that the American novel has come to the front and forced the acknowledgment of its equality with the British novel and the French novel; but for fifty years the American Short-story has had a su-

[1] It is not without interest to recall the fact that Irving's 'Sketch Book' was the earliest work of American authorship to gain popularity in Great Britain, and that it originally appeared in parts in 1819–20, — the very first part containing 'Rip van Winkle,' a perfect specimen of the American Short-story with its delightful blending of fantasy and humour. And in a letter written to a friend in New York shortly after the publication of the 'Tales of a Traveler,' in 1824, Irving pointed out, with equal shrewdness and modesty, the reasons why the Short-story seemed to him more difficult than the Novel, and also discussed his own method of composition. ('Life and Letters of Washington Irving.' New York: G. P. Putnam's Sons, 1869, vol. ii. p. 227.)

premacy which any competent critic could not but acknowledge. Indeed, the present excellence of the American novel is due in great measure to the Short-story; for nearly every one of the American novelists whose works are now read by the whole English-speaking race began as a writer of Short-stories.

Although as a form of fiction the Short-story is not inferior to the Novel, and although it is not easier, all things considered, yet its brevity makes its composition simpler for the 'prentice hand. Though the Short-stories of the beginner may not be good, yet in the writing of Short-stories he shall learn how to tell a story, he shall discover by experience the elements of the art of fiction more readily and, above all, more quickly, than if he had begun on a long and exhausting novel. The physical strain of writing a full-sized novel is far greater than the reader can well imagine. To this strain the beginner in fiction may gradually accustom himself by the composition of Short-stories.

(Here, if the digression may be pardoned, occasion serves to say that if our writers of plays had the same chance that our writers of novels have, we might now have a school of American dramatists of which we should be as proud as of our school of American novelists. In dramatic composition, the equivalent of the Short-story is the one-act play, be it drama or comedy or comedietta or farce. As the novelists have learned their trade by the writing of Short-stories, so the dramatists might learn their trade, far more difficult as it is and more complicated, by the writing of one-act plays. But, while the magazines of the United States are hungry for good Short-stories, and sift carefully all that are sent to them, in hope of happening on a treasure, the theatres of the United States are closed to one-act plays, and the dramatist is denied the opportunity of making a humble and tentative beginning. The conditions of the theatre are such that there is little hope of a change for the better in this respect, — more 's the pity. The manager has a tradition that a "broken bill," as it is called, a program containing more than one play, is a confession of weakness; — and he prefers, so far as possible, to keep his weakness concealed.)

When we read the roll of American

novelists, we see that nearly all of them began as writers of Short-stories. Some of them, Mr. Bret Harte, for instance, and Dr. Edward Everett Hale, never got any farther, or, at least, if they wrote novels, their novels did not receive the full artistic appreciation and the ample popular approval bestowed on their Short-stories. Even Mr. Cable's admirable 'Grandissimes' has not made his many readers forget his 'Posson Jone;' nor has Mr. Aldrich's 'Queen of Sheba,' charming as she is, driven from our memory his 'Margery Daw' (as delightful and as captivating as that other non-existent heroine, Mr. Austin Dobson's 'Dorothy'). Mrs. Burnett, Miss Woolson, and Miss Murfree put forth volumes of Short-stories before they attempted the more sustained flight of the full-fledged Novel. Miss Jewett, Mr. Bunner, Mr. Bishop, and Mr. Julian Hawthorne wrote Short-stories before they wrote novels; and Mr. James has never gathered into a book from the back numbers of magazines the half of his earlier efforts.[1]

[1] In the article from which a quotation has already been made (in a note on pp. 21, 22), Colonel Higginson called attention to the skill with which the local short-story in the hands of innumerable writers of both sexes in all parts of the United States has been made to yield the very form and colour of every section of our immense country; and he remarks that "the rapid multiplication of the portable kodak has scarcely surpassed the swift growth of local writers, each apparently having the same equipment of directness and vigor. All the varied elements of our society are being rapidly sought out and exhibited. To begin on the soil longest wrought, Miss Wilkins has produced a series of moral pictures, as true and as terse as anything in literature, though she has, unhappily, left rather out of sight the more cultivated and ancestral aspects of New England life, to which, however, Miss Jewett has done ampler justice."

In these references to the American magazine I believe I have suggested the real reason of the superiority of the American Short-stories over the British. It is not only that the eye of patriotism may detect more fantasy, more humour, a finer feeling for art, in these younger United States, but there is a more emphatic and material reason for the American proficiency. There is in the United States a demand for Short-stories which does not exist in Great Britain, or at any rate not in the same degree. The Short-story is of very great importance to the American magazine. But in the British magazine the serial Novel is the one thing of consequence, and all else is termed "padding." In England the writer of three-volume Novels is the best paid of literary labourers.

So it is to be noted that whoever

in England has the gift of story-telling is strongly tempted not to essay the difficult art of writing Short-stories, for which he will receive only an inadequate reward; and he is as strongly tempted to write a long story which may serve first as a serial and afterward as a three-volume Novel. The result of this temptation is seen in the fact that there is not a single British novelist whose reputation has been materially assisted by the Short-stories he has written.[1] More than once in the United States a single Short-story has made a man known; but in Great Britain such an event is well-nigh impossible. The disastrous effect on narrative art of the desire to distend every subject to

[1] Since this was written the Short-stories of R. L. Stevenson and of Mr. Kipling have proved again how dangerous it is to generalise from special conditions.

the three-volume limit has been dwelt on unceasingly by British critics.

The three-volume system is peculiar to Great Britain: it does not obtain either in France or the United States. As a consequence, the French or American writer of fiction is left free to treat his subject at the length it demands, — no more and no less. It is pleasant to note that there are signs of the beginning of the break-up of the system even in England; and the protests of the chief British critics against it are loud and frequent.[1]

It was this three-volume system which

[1] It is satisfactory to record now that the three-volume system has disappeared at last, and finally, in the years that have elapsed since this paragraph was originally penned. Its extinction moved Mr. Rudyard Kipling to chant its requiem in a series of satirical stanzas, called 'The Three-Decker,' and now to be found with his other later lyrics in 'The Seven Seas.'

was responsible in great measure for the invention and protection of the British machine for making British Novels, of which Mr. Warner told us in his entertaining essay on fiction. We all know the work of this machine, and we all recognise the trade-mark it imprints in the corner. But Mr. Warner failed to tell us, what nevertheless is a fact, that this British machine can be geared down so as to turn out the British short story. Now, the British short story, as the machine makes it and as we see it in most British magazines, is only a little British Novel, or an incident or episode from a British Novel. It is thus the exact artistic opposite of the American Short-story, of which, as we have seen, the chief characteristics are originality, ingenuity, compression, and, not infrequently, a touch of fantasy. I do not say, of course, that the good and genuine Short-story is not written in England now and then, — for if I were to make any such assertion some of the best work of Mr. Stevenson, of Mr. Besant, and of Mr. Anstey would rise up to contradict me; but this is merely an accidental growth, and not a staple of production. As a rule, in England the artist in fiction does not care to hide his light under a bushel, and he puts his best work where it will be seen of all men, — that is to say, *not* in a Short-story. So it happens that the most of the brief tales in the British magazines are not true Short-stories at all, and that they belong to a lower form of the art of fiction, in the department with the amplified anecdote. It is the three-volume Novel which has killed the Short-story in England.

Certain of the remarks in the present paper I put forth first anonymously in the columns of the *Saturday Review*, of London. To my intense surprise, they were controverted in the *Nation*, of New York.[1] The critic began by assuming that the writer had said that Americans preferred Short-stories to Novels. What had really been said was that there was a steady demand for Short-stories in American magazines, whereas in England the demand was rather for serial Novels.

"In the first place," said the critic, "Americans do not prefer Short-stories, as is shown by the enormous number of British Novels circulated among us; and in the second place, tales of the quiet,

[1] The original article will be found in the *Saturday Review* for Sept. 4, 1884; and the adverse criticism appeared in the *Nation* for July 5, 1885.

domestic kind, which form the staple of periodicals like *All the Year Round* and *Chambers's Journal*, have here thousands of readers where native productions, however clever and original, have only hundreds, since the former are reprinted by the country papers and in the Sunday editions of city papers as rapidly and regularly as they are produced at home." Now, the answer to this is simply that these British Novels and British stories are reprinted widely in the United States, not because the American people prefer them to anything else, but because, owing to the absence of international copyright, they cost nothing.[1] That the American peo-

[1] It is pleasant to be able to remark that the copyright act of 1891 removed the premium of cheapness from the British tales, and that the American writer of Short-stories is no longer compelled to produce in competition with stolen goods.

ple prefer to read American stories when they can get them is shown by the enormous circulation of the periodicals which make a speciality of American fiction.

VI

I FIND I have left myself little space to speak of the Short-story as it exists in other literatures than those of Great Britain and the United States. The conditions which have killed the Short-story in England do not obtain elsewhere; and elsewhere there are not a few good writers of Short-stories. Turgenef, Björnsen, Sacher-Masoch, Freytag, Lindau, are the names which one recalls at once and without effort as masters in the art and mystery of the Short-story. Turgenef's Short-stories, in particular, it would be difficult to commend too warmly. But it is in France that the Short-story flourishes most abundantly. In France the conditions are not unlike those in the United States; and, although there are few French magazines, there are many Parisian newspapers of a wide hospitality to literature. The demand for the Short-story has called forth an abundant supply.

Among the many excellent writers of the last generation who delighted in the *conte* — which is almost the exact French equivalent for Short-story, as *nouvelle* may be taken to indicate the story which is merely short, the episode, the incident, the amplified anecdote — were Alfred de Musset, Théophile Gautier, and Prosper Mérimée. The best work of Mérimée has never been surpassed. As compression was with him almost a mania, — as, indeed, it was with his friend Turgenef, — he seemed born on purpose to write Short-stories. Turgenef carried his desire for conciseness so far that he seems always to be experimenting to see how much of his story he may leave out.

One of the foremost writers of *contes* is Edmond About, whose charming humour is known to all readers of the 'Man with the Broken Ear'—a Short-story in conception, though unduly extended in execution. Few of the charming *contes* of M. Alphonse Daudet, or of the earlier Short-stories of M. Émile Zola, have been translated into English; and the poetic tales of M. François Coppée are likewise unduly neglected in this country. The 'Abbé Constantin' of M. Ludovic Halévy has been read by many, but the Gallic satire of his more Parisian Short-stories has been passed by, perhaps wisely, in spite of their broad humour and their sharp wit.[1] In the very singular collection of stories which M. Jean Richepin has called the 'Morts Bizarres' we find a modern continuation of the Poe tradition, always more potent in France than elsewhere.

[Here I cancel a casual sentence written in 1885, before Guy de Maupassant had completely revealed his extraordinary gifts and his marvellous craftsmanship. His Short-stories are masterpieces of the art of story-telling, because he had a Greek sense of form, a Latin power of construction, and a French felicity of style. They are

[1] In the fifteen years since this essay was first printed, this reproach has been removed, and the best of the Short-stories of Daudet, of M. Coppée and of M. Halévy have been lovingly rendered into English by American translators.

simple, most of them; direct, swift, inevitable, and inexorable in their straightforward movement. If art consists in the suppression of non-essentials, there have been few greater artists in fiction than Maupassant. In his Short-stories there is never a word wasted, and there is never an excursus. Nor is there any feebleness or fumbling. What he wanted to do he did, with the unerring certainty of Leatherstocking, hitting the bull's-eye again and again. He had the abundance and the ease of the very great artists; and the half-dozen or the half-score of his best stories are among the very best Short-stories in any language].[1]

[1] In his later tales there is to be noted a tendency towards the psychology of the morbid. The thought of death and the dread of mental disease seemed to possess him. In 'Le Horla,' for example, we find

Maupassant taking for his own Fitzjames O'Brien's uncanny monster, invisible and yet tangible; and the Frenchman gave the tale an added touch of terror by making the unfortunate victim discover that the creature he feared had a stronger will than his own, and that he was being hypnotised to his doom by a being whom he could not see, but whose presence he could feel. O'Brien's very startling tale, 'What was it?' is to be found in the volume of his Short-stories called 'The Diamond Lens' (New York: Scribner).

VII

THE Short-story should not be void or without form, but its form may be whatever the author please. He has an absolute liberty of choice. It may be a personal narrative, like Poe's 'Descent into the Maelstrom' or Mr. Hale's 'My Double, and how he Undid me'; it may be impersonal, like Mr. Frederick B. Perkins's 'Devil-Puzzlers' or Colonel J. W. De Forest's 'Brigade Commander'; it may be a conundrum, like Mr. Stockton's insoluble query, the 'Lady or the Tiger?' it may be 'A Bundle of Letters,' like Mr. Henry James's story, or 'A Letter and a Paragraph,' like Mr. Bunner's; it may be a medley of letters and telegrams and narrative, like Mr. Aldrich's

'Margery Daw'; it may be cast in any one of these forms, or in a combination of all of them, or in a wholly new form, if haply such may yet be found by diligent search. Whatever its form, it should have symmetry of design. If it have also wit or humour, pathos or poetry, and especially a distinct and unmistakable flavour of individuality, so much the better.[1] But

[1] In a chatty and somewhat uncritical paper on the 'Rise of the Short-story' contributed by Mr. Bret Harte to the 'International Library of Famous Literature' and published also in the *Cornhill Magazine* for July, 1899, we find the assertion that the secret of the American Short-story is "the treatment of characteristic American life, with absolute knowledge of its peculiarities and sympathy with its methods, with no fastidious ignoring of its national expression, or the inchoate poetry that may be found hidden even in its slang; with no moral determination except that which may be the legitimate outcome of the story itself; with no more elimination than may be necessary for the artistic conception, and never

the chief requisites are compression, originality, ingenuity, and now and again a touch of fantasy. Sometimes we may detect in a writer of Short-stories a tendency toward the over-elaboration of ingenuity, toward the exhibition of ingenuity for its own sake, as in a Chinese puzzle. But mere cleverness is incompatible with greatness, and to commend a writer as "very clever" is not to give him high praise. From this fault of supersubtlety, women are free for the most part. They are more likely than men to rely on broad human emotion, and their tendency in error is toward the morbid analysis of a high-strung moral situation.

from the fear of the fetish of conventionalism." This is cleverly phrased; but it is open to the obvious objection that it is not so much an adequate definition of the Short-story as a form as it is a defence of the special kind of Short-story Mr. Bret Harte himself has chosen to write.

VIII

THE more carefully we study the history of fiction the more clearly we perceive that the Novel and the Short-story are essentially different — that the difference between them is not one of mere length only, but fundamental. The Short-story seeks one set of effects in its own way, and the Novel seeks a wholly distinct set of effects in a wholly distinct way. We are led also to the conclusion that the Short-story — in spite of the fact that in our language it has no name of its own — is one of the few sharply defined literary forms. It is a *genre*, as M. Brunetière terms it, a species, as a naturalist might call it, as individual as the Lyric itself and as various. It is as distinct an entity as the Epic, as Tragedy, as Comedy. Now the Novel is not a form of the same sharply defined individuality; it is — or at least it may be — anything. It is the child of the Epic and the heir of the Drama; but it is a hybrid. And one of the foremost of living American novelists, who happens also to be one of the most acute and sympathetic of American critics, has told me that he was often distracted by the knowledge of this fact even while he was engaged in writing a novel.[1]

In the history of literature the Short-story was developed long before the Novel, which indeed is but a creature of yesterday, and which was not really established in popular esteem as a

1 This paragraph and the one following were not in the original essay.

worthy rival of the drama until after the widespread success of the Waverley Novels in the early years of the nineteenth century. The Short-story also seems much easier of accomplishment than the Novel, if only because it is briefer. And yet the list of the masters of the Short-story is far less crowded than the list of the masters of the longer form. There are a score or more very great novelists recorded in the history of fiction; but there are scarcely more than half a score Short-story writers of an equal eminence.

From Chaucer and Boccaccio we must spring across the centuries until we come to Hawthorne and Poe almost without finding another name that insists upon enrolment. In these five hundred years there were great novelists not a few, but there was no great writer of Short-stories. A little later than Hawthorne and Poe, and indeed almost contemporaneous with them, are Mérimée and Turgenef, whose title to be recorded there is none to dispute. Now at the end of the nineteenth century we find two more that no competent critic would dare to omit, — Guy de Maupassant and Rudyard Kipling.

Appendix

So far as the author is aware, he had no predecessor in asserting that the Short-story differs from the Novel essentially, — and not merely in the matter of length. So far as he knows, it was in the present paper the suggestion was first made that the Short-story is in reality a *genre*, a separate kind, a genus by itself. But although this distinction may not have been made explicitly by any earlier critic, there is little doubt that Poe felt it, even if he did not formulate it in set terms. It seems to be implicit in more than one of his critical essays, more particularly in that on 'Hawthorne's Tales.' And it is from this essay that the following quotations are taken: —

"The ordinary novel is objectionable from its length, for reasons already stated in substance. As it cannot be read at one sitting, it deprives itself, of course, of the immense force derivable from *totality*. Worldly interests intervening during the pauses of perusal modify, annul, or contract, in a greater or less degree, the impressions of the book. But simply cessation in reading would, of itself, be sufficient to destroy the true unity. In the brief tale, however, the author is enabled to carry out the fulness of his intention, be it what it may. During the hour of perusal the soul of the reader is at the writer's control. There are no external or extrinsic influences — resulting from weariness or interruption.

"A skilful literary artist has constructed a tale. If wise, he has not fashioned his thoughts to accommodate his incidents; but having conceived, with deliberate care, a certain unique or single *effect* to be wrought out, he then invents such incidents — he then combines such events as may best aid him in establishing this preconceived effect. If his very initial sentence tend not to the out-bringing of this effect, then he has failed in his first step.[1] In the whole composition there should be no word written of which the tendency, direct or indirect, is not to the one pre-established design. As by such means, with such care and skill, a picture is at length painted which leaves in the mind of him who contemplates it with a kindred art a sense of the fullest satisfaction. The idea of the tale has been presented unblemished, because undisturbed; and this is an end unattainable by the novel. Undue brevity is just as exceptionable here as in the poem; but undue length is yet more to be avoided."

Although no later essay has added much to our knowledge of the essential nature of

[1] It is interesting to compare what Poe says here with Stevenson's statement of the same principle already quoted in the note on page 15.

the Short-story and of its necessary characteristics, the reader may be glad to have collected here references to other attempts to deal with the subject. The most elaborate is 'Short-story Writing,' by Mr. Charles Raymond Barrett, Ph.B. (New York: The Baker and Taylor Co., 1900); of which an earlier edition had been issued by the Chicago Authors' and Writers' Union. To a little book 'On the Art of Writing Fiction' (London: Wells, Gardner Darton & Co. 1895), the authoress of 'Mademoiselle Ixe' contributed a chapter on the Short-story. 'How to write a Short-story' is the general title given to four rather personal papers by Mr. Robert Barr, Mr. Harold Frederic, Mr. Arthur Morrison, and Miss Jane Barlow, contributed to the American edition of *The Bookman* for March, 1897. To be recorded also are articles by Mr. Frederick Wedmore in the *Nineteenth Century* for March, 1898, and by Mr. Bret Harte in the *Cornhill Magazine* for July, 1899, from each of which quotation has been made in the notes on the preceding pages.

In Professor Harry Thurston Peck's exhaustive historical and critical Introduction to his vigorous and racy translation of the masterpiece of Petronius, 'Trimalchio's Dinner' (New York: Dodd, Mead & Co., 1898) there is casual mention of the Short-story as it emerges fitfully into view in Greek literature (p. 16), and in Latin (p. 40.) And in this same Introduction, Professor Peck has translated what is probably the most famous Short-story classical antiquity has bequeathed to us, — 'The Matron of Ephesus.'

Incidental discussion of the Short-story (as a form) will be found in Mr. Henry James's papers on Daudet and Maupassant and Stevenson in his 'Partial Portraits' (New York and London: Macmillan & Co.), and in my own essays on the *contes* of M. François Coppée and of M. Ludovic Halévy in 'Aspects of Fiction' (New York: Harper

& Brothers). In my Introduction to Irving's 'Tales of a Traveler' prepared for 'Longman's English classics' (edited by Professor G. R. Carpenter), there is an examination of Irving's methods and of his mastery in this difficult department of the art of narrative. There is also a brief but admirable essay by Mr. Henry Harland in the London *Academy* for June 5th, 1897.

An interesting international comparison can be had by setting side by side the specimens of this art contained in three series, of ten volumes each, published by Chas. Scribner's Sons, — 'Stories by American Authors,' 'Stories by English Authors,' and 'Stories by Foreign Authors.' The second series had better have been called 'Stories by British Authors,' since it contained also the work of Scotchmen and Irishmen. The English and Foreign series are each representative of the best the authors of the several countries have to show; but the American series — excellent as it is — does not thus present the pick of American Short-story writing, since the editor limited his own freedom of choice by selecting from the magazines only those stories which the authors had not yet re-plevined for volumes of their own.

Lightning Source UK Ltd.
Milton Keynes UK
UKOW010416071112

201738UK00004B/60/P